tiny ruins

Editor: Elizabeth Philips
Cover art: Zachari Logan
Book and cover design: Tania Wolk, Third Wolf Studio
Printed and bound in Canada at Friesens, Altona, MB

The publisher gratefully acknowledges the support of Creative Saskatchewan, the Canada Council for the Arts and SK Arts.

Library and Archives Canada Cataloguing in Publication

Title: Tiny ruins / Nicole Haldoupis.
Other titles: Tiny ruins (2020)
Names: Haldoupis, Nicole, 1990- author.
Identifiers: Canadiana (print) 20200303546 | Canadiana (ebook) 20200303554 | ISBN 9781989274385 (softcover) | ISBN 9781989274392 (PDF)
Classification: LCC PS8615.A38576 T55 2020 | DDC C813/.6—dc23

radiant press
Box 33128 Cathedral PO
Regina, SK S4T 7X2
info@radiantpress.ca
www.radiantpress.ca

tiny ruins

nicole haldoupis

for Big D and Clark

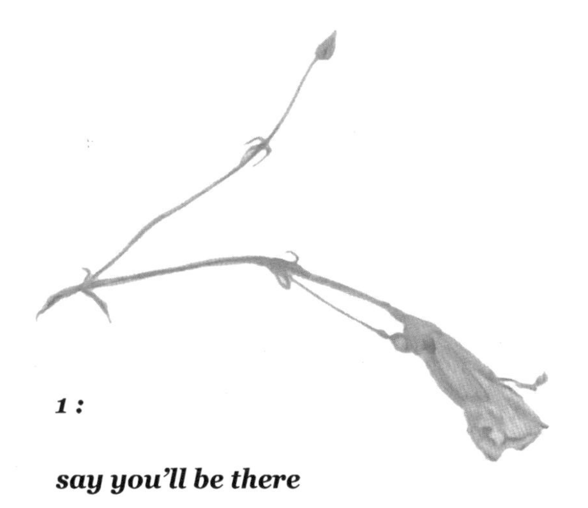

say you'll be there

Robin

A baby bird fell from the birch tree in the front yard in the spring. Alana watched her big sister Janie and their mother dig gardening gloves out of the garage, and she crouched close as Janie picked up the baby. They kept it in the hanging plant on the front porch so cats couldn't reach it. The mother robin perched on the edge of the planter and the baby bird ate from her beak. The girls and their mother watched through the window and the mother bird watched back. When she left, the girls took the chirping baby down. Alana cupped it in gloved hands. The baby flapped its wings. It didn't fly, but it tried. So Alana bounced her hands up and down and the bird flapped its wings, landing gentler every time. After a few days, Janie and Alana were tossing the bird five feet into the air and it would flutter before falling safe into their palms. Every day it stayed up a little longer. One day they saw the mother robin watching from the fence, and when Janie and Alana put the baby robin back into its hanging plant, she fed it.

Soon the robin was flying higher than ever. Janie put the baby on the grass for a moment and, when she turned away, Sean the cat wobbled over. The baby chirped from between Sean's teeth. Janie, Alana, and their mother screamed. Chased the cat all the way to the neighbour's backyard, but he had already scooted far under the porch. Sean chomped and the baby bird chirped, and then stopped chirping. Later, Sean scratched and meowed at the door and Janie and Alana's mother yelled at him to go away. Janie wouldn't come out of her and Alana's bedroom, and Alana built a Lego forest on the living room carpet. She looked out the window and saw the mother robin waiting.

Tough Pants

Mary, with the brown bowl cut and the squeaky voice, was their leader. She gathered everyone into a circle in the schoolyard by the far end of the track, near the dumpsters. The wind blew her hair in choppy sections as she stood high on the cement hill.

"Okay, someone smells like poo!" Mary announced.

Another girl chimed in, "I smelled it too, way back there," and gestured to the grassy corner where they were playing an hour ago.

All the other little girls nodded in agreement, and a few uttered a "yeah," or, "it does smell like poop!"

Alana stood in the circle and agreed with the other girls, her pants filled with poop from her accident earlier in the day. She didn't know how to deal with pooping in a toilet without help from her mother. No one seemed to notice that the smell was coming from her, and she was determined to keep it that way as long as possible, maybe even forever.

"Okay, we're gonna do a vote," Mary decided. "So, whoever didn't poop their pants, say 'I' at the count of three. One, two, three—"

Every single little girl in the group, including Alana, chimed in with an "I" in unison, loud enough to make the older kids on the jungle gym look over to see what they were doing. None of the other little girls found out who pooped their pants that day. Alana went home in the afternoon and sobbed her way to the bathroom where her mother helped her clean up.

Lava Rug River, Wine Mountain

They crawled along a wooden plank, red-orange rug of molten lava bubbling inches beneath their palms. They gripped engraved pillars to keep steady, thumbing grooves. Rug-burnt knees slipped, hands stumbled around large socked feet, uncles grumbled. They played cards on the table over their heads with cartoon knights and horses. Not regular playing cards: Sicilian cards, with men holding secret meanings in sword sheaths. Nonno scratched lottery tickets while Nonna sang shaky songs in the kitchen.

The girls hopped on cardboard box lids, clung to each other. Searched for a lava-proof paddle. Climbing carboys in the closet, they scaled wicker-wrapped terrain with no harness in the dark. Wine thief snake threatened to strike, red drops down its throat straight into its belly. Hearing their names called, they peered through the shutters.

Flowers

Mother buys flowers for herself every week and puts them in a vase. If there wasn't so much snow outside, Alana would walk—but not past the end of the driveway—and pick all the flowers she could find for her. One night, she woke up crying, Janie fast asleep across the room. She went to her mother's bed and said "Mama I don't want to get reborn as a flower or a bee or anyone because then you wouldn't be my mama" and her mother touched her face and said "oh sweetie" and Alana cried and her mother carried her back to her bed and she fell asleep, as if it never happened.

Neopets

Sara and Janie shared the computer chair while Alana spied outside the door. They took turns feeding their neopets after trips to the giant omelette to grab a slice. Some omelettes were more rare than others, but they fed them all to their virtual pets regardless of value. Alana opened the door enough for Sean to squeeze through. He meowed and landed with a thump on the desk and clumsily walked across the keyboard as the girls scrambled to move him so he wasn't blocking their pets on-screen. He whined as Janie placed him on the ground.

"Sean's kinda dumb, isn't he?" said Sara.

Janie shrugged. "He's not that smart I guess."

"Does he even cuddle?"

"Yeah, he cuddles a lot."

"My cat Salem is the best cuddler."

Janie fed omelettes to her blue dragon neopet.

"Can I play too?" Alana asked as she walked in.

"No, Alana, go away," said Janie.

Alana picked up Sean, almost half her size, and they left the room.

Hair

Rachel pulled Janie's hair. It was the third time Alana saw her do it this week. Grabbed a tangle at the top and yanked until Janie's eyes watered. Janie tried to pull Rachel's hands off her, but Rachel had a good grip. Janie just had to wait for her to stop. Other kids played around them. Janie pulled Tommy's hair and he said "Ow! Stop!" so she did. Alana watched as Janie sat down on the concrete hill. Alana didn't sit with her. Not even the teachers noticed. Janie sat on the hill and watched the other kids running around, studied the concrete around her feet.

Midsummer

Janie, Alana, and their mother stayed at a cottage they rented up north for a week every summer. After dark one night, the adults took the kids into the woods. The girls followed the flashlight across the pine needle floor through trees that all looked the same. They held hands to stay close. Usually there was nothing to do at night except watch movies or play board games, since they weren't allowed outside without an adult. In the day they could play in the stream, around the pool filled with turtles, go to the beach if their mother felt like it. Janie and Alana spent a lot of time together. They didn't know the other kids. They were too scared to talk to them. Some of the littler kids stayed near them on their walk but the bigger kids ranged ahead. They had been there before and knew where they were going in the dark. One of the adults said to make sure to say hello when they get there. Alana said, "to who?" The woman shone her flashlight down to her left. A gravestone shone back.

Live in There

Alana leaned into the fire almost too warm on her toes but her uncle kept telling stories and she needed to hear the end of this one. He had a real spooky voice, not like when people try to have a spooky voice but it doesn't work. His was spooky for real. She could tell he'd been practicing.

"The little girl wandered into the dark woods," he gestured towards the trees behind them.

"Then what happened!" her cousin Jack could barely keep his bum on the tree stump.

"It was quiet—a little too quiet..."

Alana started feeling sleepy. She leaned into the warmth of the fire, felt the pressure of the edge of her chair as her bum fell asleep. With her feet resting on the stones around the pit, she watched an ant climb into the fire, stop, change colour from black to red, and burn. She wondered what it'd be like to live in there.

Sister Games

Charlie was the prince and Janie was the princess and he chased her around the schoolyard trying to kiss her and she screamed and ran away. Alana watched and cried. Every time. Charlie explained: “It’s just a game.” Alana cried harder.

One day, Alana dug in the sandbox by herself while they played, and she didn’t cry. She saw Janie spin around looking for her, saw Charlie catch her and wrap his arms around her like a slack rope. They glared at each other. Janie pushed him off and ran to Alana.

“Charlie caught me,” Janie said.

Alana looked up at her, continued digging.

“Let’s play a game,” Janie declared.

Alana handed her a blue plastic shovel.

Janie's Cat

Hi, Janie.

The receiver was too large for Janie's palm, so the corners dug into her fingers. Alana sat close enough to hear the voice on the other end, watched the plastic press into Janie's cheek, the phone cord squiggling to the wall. "Hi Sara. I can't talk to you."

Why not?

"Mom says you're a negative influence in my life and I shouldn't talk to you anymore."

Oh but, Janie, wait—um, your cat, you know your cat?

"Yeah."

He's dead, Janie. I went for a walk around the block from your house and he's on the road, he's dead. Someone ran him over, Janie.

Janie squeezed the hard plastic, slipping in her hand now. "I can't talk to you, Sara."

But, Janie, your cat. Just walk around the block, Janie.

"Bye Sara."

Janie, wait—

Dandelion

Alana held on to him tight like one of those koala toys her uncle brought from Australia last Christmas, the one that wears a vest and hugs tight to her little finger. Jeremy squirmed and said, "Let me go!" three times and then yelled, "I'm married to Rebecca!" Alana looked down the running track in the schoolyard and saw Rebecca watching them, arms crossed, angry-faced, like she wouldn't talk to her for a few weeks. Jeremy flailed to get away but couldn't. "Um, we're married," Rebecca said as she walked up to them. Alana remembered their wedding ceremony, under the mulberry bush at lunch recess on the grassy hill that turned into an ice slide in the winter. Their wedding day was sunny with a berry feast, purple squished onto the bottoms of their shoes. Still she held tight and didn't let Jeremy go. She wanted him to hug her like he hugged Rebecca, round the waist under the mulberry branches so they could take wedding pictures. She thought if she held him tight enough he might stay and she wouldn't have to walk around the track alone anymore. She closed her eyes and made a wish in her head as she squeezed: *I wish Jeremy would marry me under the mulberry tree*, and then she let go. He ran, not to Rebecca but far down the track until she didn't know where. Rebecca turned away too, walked the other way. Alana stood alone. Dandelion seeds floated in the air.

Rebecca Farted

The kitchen reeked of frying garlic and butter as Alana sauntered in with Sean in her arms. Sean whined and wriggled, his claws against her T-shirt, and Alana put him down next to her mother, in front of the stove.

"Guess what, Mama?"

"What is it, honey?" Alana's mother pushed the sizzling garlic around and it crackled in the pan.

"Rebecca farted at school today."

Alana walked out of the room.

Black Hole

"I'm scared about what happens after you die. Is it just a black hole forever, or..." Alana was on the phone with a Kids Help Phone agent. She had questions she was too nervous to ask anyone else and thought maybe the lady on the phone could provide the answers she was looking for.

Alana often imagined what it would be like to be dead. She closed her eyes and was floating through space, except there were no stars or planets or anything pretty, nothing but darkness. No parties with dead pets and relatives in the clouds, no coming back to life as a bird or any other animal she might like to be one day. She imagined being stuck with nothing for the rest of time–she blinked and it was black and she opened her eyes and it was also black. The boredom she anticipated for the rest of eternity made her panic until she fell asleep.

"You're so cute!"

Alana felt her breathing speed up, sniffled. "But, will it be like that forever? I need to know what really happens."

"Aw, are you crying? You're so sweet. I wish you were my daughter!"

"I have to go... my mom's home." Alana hung up the phone.

Four Flutes

Brassy squawks erupted from inside the classroom. Janie told Alana she'd walked in behind Charlie, the freckly boy she couldn't stop staring at whenever she got the chance. She hoped no one was looking, but it was hard to tell sometimes. She wanted to play the saxophone because it was handsome and sounded different from all of the other instruments. She wasn't sure though. Most of the other girls wanted to play the flute, because it was small and pretty. She sat beside Charlie and looked at the freckle near his mouth that moved when he smiled.

"What do you want to play?" he asked her.

"I don't know, what do you want to play?"

"I think I want to play the sax."

"Me too!" She was so excited about learning the saxophone, just her and Charlie. Thought maybe they could meet up at each other's houses after school to practice. The teacher went around the room, writing down the students' choices.

"Sax!" yelled Charlie.

"Me too!" Janie said.

"I'm afraid we only have one alto sax. One of you will need to pick something else."

They looked at each other. Charlie's freckle returned to its original spot.

"The clarinet is similar to learn," the teacher told them.

They looked at each other again, knowing how much the other wanted to play the sax.

"I'll play clarinet, I guess," offered Janie.

The teacher scribbled on his clipboard and assigned her a clarinet number to retrieve from the pile. Charlie ran to the only saxophone case in the room. Janie walked over to the clarinet pile and then to the clarinet section, sat in her black folding chair, next to the girls who wanted to play the flute.

Climbing Trees

Alana climbed the tree out front as she waited for Janie to get home. Janie was at Charlie's house and Alana knew she had a crush on Charlie. She made Alana swear never to tell their mother, because then she wouldn't let her go to his house again. Alana asked Janie if Charlie was her boyfriend and if they were going to get married but Janie said no. Alana never had a boyfriend, but she was friends with boys in her class. Some of them climbed the tree behind the portables with her when the teacher wasn't looking, and they asked her what the other girls' favourite colours were. She always told them "brown" even though it wasn't true.

From the tree in front of their house, Alana saw Janie walking with Charlie. Alana's glasses slipped down her nose and she couldn't push them back because she needed her hands to hold onto the tree, so she had to squint through the branches at her sister twirling her clarinet case and staring at Charlie. They stopped when they got close to the house and Alana pushed her glasses back with a branch, stretched so she could put her face through the leaves, and next thing she was on the ground screaming and Janie and their mother ran to her.

Now she's stuck at home with her mother and Sean the cat and a cast on her leg that her toes poke out of. Sean sleeps on her legs and licks her toes. She can't wait in trees for Janie anymore, she can't see what her and Charlie do on their walk home. All she can do is watch her sister's face when she gets home, ask when they're getting married.

Chicken Nuggets

Janie told Alana later that she'd been wandering the aisles of folding tables in the hall, touched all the books without really looking. She had been by herself because Sara was mad at her for some reason. Alana's class wasn't going to the book fair until the afternoon. Sara hadn't talked to Janie in nearly a week. Janie visited Sara a lot on the weekends, and sometimes Alana came too, but they didn't go last weekend. Salem the cat usually hid the whole time and Sara's mom made chicken nuggets and French fries in the oven because that's what Sara wanted. They'd dip them in ketchup as they sat together on the couch watching a movie. Sara and Alana liked scary movies but Janie usually kept her eyes closed.

Janie said she picked up a Spice Girls book, and the girls on the other side of the book table giggled as they flipped through a shiny Leonardo DiCaprio book. Janie was studying the pictures of Ginger, Baby, Sporty, Scary, and Posh when Sara grabbed her arm and said, "I'm not mad at you anymore, come look at this!" Sara brought her to the dog book section and showed her a book with a German shepherd on the cover that looked just like her dog Chester.

"I'm trying to find a cat book with a cat that looks like Salem too, but I can't find one," said Sara.

"Did you see the book with the chicken nuggets on the cover?"

"I need that book! This is why we're friends."

Janie took Sara to the chicken nugget book and then Ms. D called them back in for French class.

Hard Winter

Janie didn't know how hard it had been, she told Alana, until the sun came out and she had to take off her coat on the way home from school because it was too hot. Other kids ran in the schoolyard and she ran too and launched her arms toward the sun and reached until she felt like she was getting close. Charlie smiled at her like she'd never seen him smile before. He'd been sick that winter and was home from school for three weeks. They had indoor recess because it was too cold, and Sara got mad at her a lot and didn't speak to her for weeks. She couldn't even go to the classroom next door to see Alana because that wasn't allowed. Janie said she would sit and wait for the days to be over, read books in her lap so the teacher couldn't see. Charlie passed notes and made her giggle in secret but when he was away no one passed her notes. But, she told Alana, he was back now, and she could run and smile in the sun.

Pink Jar

Alana sometimes imagined sitting on top of Sara and washing her face. Sara lying on her back on the bathroom floor, and Alana, tiles cold on her knees, scrubbing to get all the gunk out because Sara didn't know how. Not properly, anyway. Alana would use her favourite face wash, the one that smells like lemon and makes lots of bubbles, lathering all over until it seemed like she was lathering too long. Then she'd get a washcloth and start scrubbing—she'd scrub in circles, getting off all the dead skin so Sara's face would be shiny and smooth when they rinsed with cold water, pores closing tight like *Cosmo Girl* said. Then they'd moisturize—she'd use her pink jar of face cream that she only picked because it was on sale even though she hates pink. Alana told her mother and she said it was a silly idea, that Sara probably didn't need her help. Alana explained how she would do it and her mother went back to reading her book. "Just forget about it," she'd said, "she can figure it out for herself."

The Girl with Shit in Her Hair

Alana watched Sara's long hair tangling, the wind causing stubby knots that her mother would later yank out with a brush. They ran between the two football posts no one used for football. They were chasing one another, no boys allowed. The boys tried to jump in and chase too sometimes, but the girls stood still and watched them until they left—it didn't take long. Alana had glimpsed something that was maybe some cat shit in the corner of the field. The girls all stopped to look. Sara almost ran into it, grabbed Alana's arm to steady herself. Her hand was clammy from clenching her fists while running, tiny hands like a troll doll's. Alana leaned into her touch.

Someone had stepped in the shit, but they didn't know who. One of them, or another kid in the playground? One of the boys, maybe, or one of the small kids? She saw Jeremy pointing and laughing. His long hair didn't tangle easily because it was thick, not like Sara's. Alana liked when he smiled at her, though he didn't do it very often. But he gave Sara a Valentine's card this year—pink with a green spotted dinosaur that said, "'Rawr' means 'I Love You' in Dinosaur." So he must like her, Alana thought.

"Who stepped in shit?" asked Jackie.

"Janie's got shit on her hands!" they heard a boy yell—it was Jeremy. "It's in her hair! Ew!" All the boys laughed as Janie began to yowl. Her hair smeared with brown near the top—she must have scratched her head with her shitty hand. The teachers on recess duty stood near the fence and chatted, while Janie stood with her hand frozen in the air, shit smeared on her palm, in her hair, who knows where else. Alana watched from the field as Sara ran over and whispered to Janie, who sniffled and nodded. They turned and walked together towards the school.

“I wonder how she got the shit on her hands,” Jackie speculated.

“Probably fell or something,” said Florence.

“And didn’t even notice? I feel like I would notice.”

Alana watched Sara’s green pants scrunch behind the knees as she walked, hand on Janie’s back. She watched Jeremy snickering to his friends, still pointing. He turned to look at Alana. His eyes sparkled and the side of his mouth crinkled up at her.

Twist

Alana sat on the concrete hill. The boys were running around pushing each other to the ground, and Sara was braiding Janie's hair. Sara she picked a dandelion and tucked it into a fold of braid. Janie felt the flower with her hand and smiled. Rebecca was showing some of the other girls how to do a dance. The girls had never seen anything like it—she slapped her thigh, twisted her arms in the air—said her cousin was a dancer in music videos. The girls watched her body move and attempted to copy her, their brows twisted in knots. Unison wasn't achieved. The boys started running in circles around Janie and Sara, kicking dirt as they went. Janie held her hands over her face as Sara stood up and pushed the boys away, singling out Jeremy because he was the leader.

"What's your problem?" she said.

Jeremy laughed as the other boys jostled each other. "We're just playing around."

"You're bullying her for no reason," she said and gestured at Janie.

"I'm not the one who put shit in my own hair." The boys roared.

"Get a life, Jeremy." Sara took Janie by the arm and they walked towards the bushes, brushing dirt out of their eyes.

Old Songs

When they started playing them, the tunes that came out when she was four, the ones her older cousins would listen to that made her aunt say *don't let the girls listen to those*, Alana started thinking about asking Sara. In the foggy gymnasium full of grades six-to-eight, a few boys and girls were slow dancing, keeping almost a foot between them, except for Rebecca and Jeremy who nuzzled each other in front of everyone until a teacher went and talked to them and they stopped. Alana watched for Sara in the dark gym, saw her talking to the other girls, tugging at Janie's arms, trying to convince her to dance when a fast song came on. Janie was too nervous to dance, much like Alana was too nervous to move. She saw Sara go to the bathroom. She should go now—now was her chance. But she couldn't bring herself to walk towards the door, go through it, down the hall, into the bathroom, see Sara standing in front of the mirror reapplying her shiny lip gloss that she only wore at school dances. Then what? Sara would say *let's go see who we can slow dance with* but it was boys she meant so Alana would have to tell her, *I want to dance with you.*

Shade

"This is Conor," Alana said, "he's my boyfriend."

"Hi Conor," Janie said.

Conor stared.

"Um, what's your favourite colour?"

"Black," Conor said, without a smile.

"That's not a colour, it's all colours mixed together."

Conor didn't reply.

Janie walked away.

Somewhere Near Danforth

Alana snooped in Janie's diary: *Your lip does this thing sometimes where it curls down when you think no one is looking at you and you stare off into space or at the TV or the wall or wherever it is you're looking. I've learned not to interrupt you.*

I imagine us living on the top floor of a building with an outdoor pool we don't swim in because it smells like piss.

Sometimes your eyes look sad, but I know you're not really sad. You just have sad eyes sometimes. I know how to change them back now.

We'll have a balcony and we'll sit on it every morning and drink coffee and watch the steam and smog and clouds swirling and blending over the city.

Small Turtles

The cabin was unusually quiet, just the sound of the waves through the open window when Janie and Alana woke up to find their mother gone. She'd woken them up at seven in the morning to say she'd be going out for groceries and other supplies for the family reunion and would be back in about two hours. It had been five. She'd probably gotten caught up shopping.

"Do we have any food?" asked Alana.

"I think I left a granola bar in the car..." answered Janie.

Their stomachs growled as they walked through the pines behind the cabin to distract themselves from their hunger. They followed a familiar path, crossed at the low part of the creek and found themselves in the grassy clearing. The abandoned wooden ski chalet, falling apart, gaped at them through shattered windows. A snake looked at them and they looked at it and it didn't flinch when they waved. Alana thought it might be dead.

The swimming pool in the back had filled with green water over several seasons. Small turtles raced each other and clung to logs and car tires.

They searched for open windows and doors every time they visited the chalet, but they were always locked. They tried the door on the side of the building, like they had many times before.

This time the door opened.

In the Chalet

A toque and a pair of pants on the floor signalled that someone besides them had been there. Pamphlets on safe skiing were scattered across the welcome desk, smiling skiers in eighties gear splashed over them. Decades-old pop bottles, a teacup filled with ashes, and cigarette butts littered the carpet behind the desk.

They found the room they saw through the window outside, a time capsule preserving the chaos of the day they closed down. Maps and plans and files and Post-its and a cheque for $29.99 made out to some guy named Dave and a photo envelope lay on the desk of someone who'd left that last day.

They stood in the lobby. Down the hallway, doors were ajar. They could see the stairs leading up to another level of dust, thought they heard creaking. They didn't go upstairs.

A statue of someone, Jesus or some saint no taller than a thumb, lay sideways on a window ledge to bid farewell.

Frog Girl

The little girl squinted in the sun, grabbed a frog out of the long grass. "This is Alana," Maddie said.

"Oh, I'm flattered," said human Alana.

"She's not named after you." Maddie shot Alana a dirty look. "I always wanted to be a frog. Because I'm a princess, so then one day a prince will kiss me, and I'll become handsome."

"That's a nice twist on the story!"

The girl looked at Alana like she was the dumbest person she'd ever met, then gently placed the frog on the grassy shoreline. Waves drove a dead fish repeatedly into the rocks an arm's length away. "You have a fat bum," Maddie said. "Why is her bum fat?" she yelled to her mother—a cousin Alana had met earlier that day—as she approached them from the cabin.

Maddie's mother eyed her child in surprise, shifted her feet in the grass. She looked at Alana and laughed nervously.

Alana turned her attention to the clovers in the lawn, the green circles of them overwhelming her vision. When Alana had found her first four-leaf clover she was around the same age as the little girl. She thought she'd get marshmallows or gold out of it, but she didn't get anything, just a feeling of being lucky, and that hadn't lasted. She'd found a bunch more since then and wasn't sure if it was because she was lucky or because she spent too much time staring at the ground.

Maddie put her lifejacket on, bat symbol drawn on the back in permanent marker, and stuck one foot in the canoe. She crouched and clutched the sides when the boat wobbled and she stayed like that for the rest of the ride. Maddie's mom got in the back so Alana got in the front, even though she was reluctant to reveal her ass to the little girl again in case she had more comments.

"Mommy, my friend told me that boys like when girls have big bums."

Alana rolled her eyes so only the ducks ahead of them could see.

"Sweetie, I don't think we should talk about bums anymore."

"I wasn't!"

Alana paddled on the right side for a while, then switched to the left.

Bees

Alana climbed out of the canoe, placed her bare foot in the grass. Maddie stuck out her hand and held onto the side with the other, yelled "Mommy help me!" Alana braced the boat against the shore while Maddie's mom helped her to get out, mouthed a sympathetic "thank you" at Alana for keeping an eye on the child, then rushed back to the cabin to make dinner with Alana's mother. Alana dragged the canoe far enough onto the shore so it didn't float away.

"I want to find more frogs." Maddie glared at Alana.

Alana sat on the grass.

"Why are you sitting there?" The girl combed through the tall grass, dragged up a slimy pile of something from the water—not a frog.

"Because it's comfortable."

The girl wiped her hands on her lifejacket, and then sat down a few feet away. A bee hovered near her, riffling through flower petals in the grass before moving on. The girl leaned away from it.

"What if my bum gets dirty?" Maddie asked.

"It'll be fine."

"Can I see yours?"

"No."

The little girl shrank away when the bee tumbled closer, sipping from a yellow flower. The bee rose up and Maddie shrieked. "Why won't it go away?"

"It's not going to hurt you." Alana smiled and tickled the girl's leg with a blade of grass. Maddie jumped at her touch and yelled again while the bee hovered calmly.

Fourteen

Alana heard Janie on the phone in their room. "Of course I remember the first time you kissed me. You were nervous and I was nervous and I said 'Charlie, just do it,' and then you did. I grabbed your shirt to pull you closer because I didn't want you to stop and you didn't get too close because you had a boner and didn't want me to know. Then you stopped and I said, 'You missed,' but you didn't miss. I just wanted you to do it again."

Evil Eye

Alana had period cramps and a headache.

"You have the malocchio," her grandmother said. "That's why your head hurts."

"No, Nonna. I'm bleeding from my vagina."

Her mother gave her a look.

"We have to see how many little devils," her nonna said.

Alana sighed.

The two women sat her on a chair, wrapped a towel around her shoulders and clipped it in front with a clothespin. Her mother fetched a bottle of olive oil while her nonna filled a large mixing bowl with water and held it to rest on top of her head.

Her mother poured oil into the bowl and they both stood over her and watched.

"Madonna!" her nonna said. Her mother gave a worried-yet-guilt-trippy gasp and threw her hand over her mouth. Her mother walked back into the kitchen to find salt, handed it to her nonna, and took over holding the bowl. Her nonna poured salt into her hand and threw it in the bowl to burn the evil eyes.

"There, your head will feel better now," her nonna said, as she and her mother unpinned the towel and then took the bowl and salt back to the kitchen.

"Thanks, Nonna," Alana said, and walked slowly upstairs to take some Advil.

Naked with Sara

Alana found a pack of gum in her bag that had probably been there for months and popped a piece into her mouth. It went from hard and minty to soft and tasteless within seconds. She hoped the mint would stand in for brushing her teeth, and that with her messy bun, she'd look showered.

She ran into Sara on the subway. Sara knew when Alana's hair was up it meant she hadn't showered.

"I didn't get any homework done last night," Sara said. "Miss Evans is gonna be pissed."

"True, I just had a bit of math."

"It smells like puke in here. Wanna come over after school?"

Alana tried not to think about the dream where she was naked with Sara and on top of her and Sara let her kiss her neck and suck on her earlobes and then giggled and then they showered separately. Sara had never suggested she was interested in girls—neither had Alana—and Alana had no idea where the dream came from, but she wanted it to happen again. She wanted to be naked with Sara but knew she probably never would be and she could never tell anyone.

Power Rangers

Alana wore her kilt longer than everyone else. Girls made fun of her and told her she needed to hike it up. When she rolled it short her butt made it stick out and reveal her Power Rangers boxers to everyone. Teachers got mad at her and boys stared at her and it wasn't even as short as the other girls', it was just because of her bum. She thought about Maddie's big bum comments at the lake and decided to wear pants that day.

"It's summer," Sara said. "Why are you wearing pants?"

"It's not that hot out," Alana answered.

Other girls had their kilts hiked and shirts tied up around their bellies to allow airflow. Alana undid her pants and rolled them over her hips because it was less restricting than having them tight around her waist, then pulled her shirt down to cover the arrangement. Before Janie and Sara went to class, they lowered their shirts back over their midriffs and unrolled their kilts so they were just the right length for their science teacher, who was strict about kilt length. Alana was happy she didn't have to worry about that with her less strict teacher, and she marched into class like she was dressed to kill.

"Alana, can you tuck in your shirt please?" the teacher said.

Alana sighed and lifted her shirt to tuck. When the teacher saw Alana's pants rolled down, revealing her underwear, she shook her head and walked away. Alana tucked in her shirt, did up her pants, and sat through class, her stomach aching.

The Catcher

During lunch at school, Alana sat on the dusty tiles next to Sara in the hallway. Sara and Janie had gotten into a fight and weren't talking, and Janie spent her lunches canoodling with Charlie in various hidden places in the school. Alana wanted to see what Sara was reading, but Sara noticed her staring and said "what?" and Alana just looked away.

Sara poked Alana's shoulder and said, "Can I talk to you?" and she thought she was going to invite her for a sleepover. Alana started breathing heavier and getting hot and probably red and Sara said, "Are you okay?" Alana said yeah and shook her hair out from behind her ears, covering the half of her face closest to Sara. Sara asked her if she wanted to walk home together because she was nervous Evan was going to try to walk with her again and he'd creeped her out the other day when he'd followed her all the way to her house and asked if they could hang out. He was a really touchy guy, always finding an excuse to put his sweaty hands on her, she said, and she really didn't want to hang out with him so she lied and said she couldn't because her mom was home.

Alana walked Sara home and all the way there she thought about asking if she wanted to hang out after but got nervous because she didn't want to be another creepy guy for her except a girl this time. She worried maybe then they couldn't be friends anymore. Sara asked if she was okay because she wasn't talking and Alana said yeah, slid her hair behind her ear. Sara asked if Alana wanted to hang out. Her mom had made cupcakes. "Shouldn't we wait until after dinner?" Alana asked, and Sara rolled her eyes.

Their arms were touching while they read and ate cupcakes in bed. Sara was reading *Angus, Thongs and Full-*

Frontal Snogging and Alana was reading *The Catcher in the Rye* for school. Alana kept getting distracted thinking about the dream she'd had, tried to get rid of the thought.

"Have you read this?" Alana asked.

"Yeah, I loved it!"

"I'm loving it too." Alana found it kind of pretentious so far.

Was it starting to rain? No, it was just the sprinkler set up too close to the window. The water hit the glass for a few seconds then rotated away.

Shine

The boys stood at the bus stop in front of the bench and talked loudly and looked at Alana and Sara every time the girls giggled about something. They all got on the bus, got off at Coxwell Station, got on the subway train. The girls whispered and looked at the boys. The boys got off the train at their usual stop.

"I know they want to be our friends," said Sara, sitting up straight in her seat, "I can tell. I think we'll be friends one day."

Sara and Alana had stayed on longer than necessary to be near the boys just in case they spoke to them, then took a bus back to Coxwell and went home from there.

"I think we'll definitely be friends with them," Alana agreed. "Is it dumb that we do this? Janie always says this is dumb."

"It isn't dumb! It gives us more time to talk after school, anyway."

"They did look at us when we mentioned going to the beach this weekend."

At Coxwell, Florence and some of the preppy kids approached Sara and Alana. Florence rolled her kilt up after school and didn't wear shorts underneath, so you could kind of see her butt when she walked in front of you.

"Hi Florence!" said Sara. Alana smiled with her mouth closed to hide her braces.

"Sara! My parents are going to be at the cottage this weekend," said Florence, "so I was going to have a few people over." The other preppy girls snickered behind her. "Do you want to come?"

"That sounds like fun!" Sara said. Florence had naturally straight teeth and Sara had already gotten her braces off, so she also had perfect teeth. Their teeth shone at each other.

When Florence and her friends walked away, Sara said, “What should we wear? Do you wanna go shopping tomorrow?”

“Florence didn’t invite me,” Alana said.

“She asked if we wanted to come, both of us.”

“She said *you*. She was looking at you. She didn’t even say hi to me.”

“I’m sure it’s fine.”

“I don’t really want to go anyway.”

Rabbit

Janie and Alana were sleeping over at their nonna's and were preparing to watch her VHS copy of *Alice in Wonderland.* They set up the pullout couch in the basement—tossed the cushions aside, unfolded the creaky mattress, and arranged sheets, blankets, and pillows on the bed. Sean the cat, who they brought along for the night, had snuggled into the pillows before they could lie down, so to get comfortable they had to awkwardly prop themselves up around him. Their nonna checked to see if they needed anything before she went to sleep, but they were ready—tucked in with the hot orange rug glowing like lava below as they sailed into their childhood.

When they reached the part where Alice shrinks herself to follow the white rabbit, Alana asked, "Can I tell you something?"

"What?" Janie didn't take her eyes away from the TV as a giant Alice cried.

"I don't know, it's silly never mind."

"Just tell me!"

"I... guess I had a dream? About Sara?"

"And?"

"I don't know..."

"Just watch the movie."

"We were naked."

Janie looked at her sister. "And?"

"I think I like her, that's all."

"What do you mean?"

Alana pulled the blankets up to her eyes. "I mean... I think I have a crush on her."

Janie blinked. "It was just a dream, Alana."

"No but, in real life too."

“You and Sara were naked in real life?”

“No! No. I just…”

“What?”

“Want to be?”

“It’s because of the dream. Maybe you wanna be like her. It’s not a crush.”

“How do you know?”

Janie turned back to the movie. “Just stop thinking about it.”

Sean purred, nuzzling Alana’s face as she stared at the TV. Maybe Janie was right.

On the screen, Alice searched for the white rabbit.

rush of blood to the head

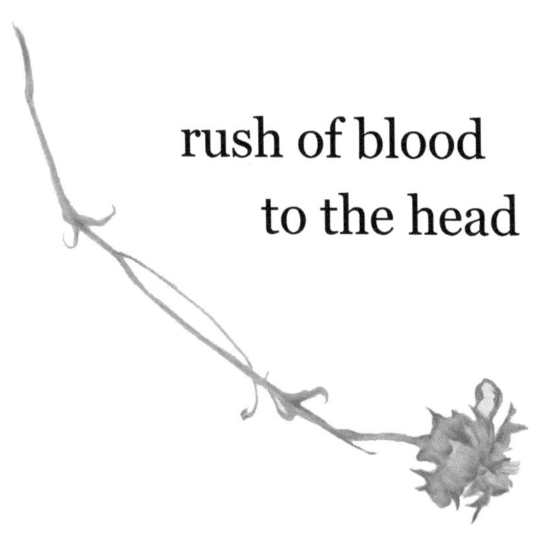

No One Writes on the First Page

Alana let the door of her sister's room in their basement apartment creak open and peered inside, making sure no one was there even though she knew Janie would be at her economics lecture for at least another hour. After their fight the night before, Alana wanted to know if Janie had written about her in her notebook.

She tiptoed into the room, making sure not to touch anything in case Janie had set a trap for her, placing objects strategically so she could evaluate when she got home if they had been moved, whether her sister had snuck in.

Alana thumbed through a pile of papers on the edge of her desk, a draft of an essay on some economic theory. Walked to her dresser, to the chair piled high with clothes worn but not yet dirty, and found no notebook. She arrived at her night table, books strewn about, including a worn copy of *The Godfather*, open with pages pressed down, and economics textbooks, spines yet to be cracked. Then she saw it—the plain black cover, pen tucked into the coil. Corner poking out from under the blue sky of a McGraw-Hill hardcover. Alana pried the notebook out, trying not to disturb the books around it. She opened the cover to find nothing on the first page, but Janie told her that no one writes on the first page, so she flipped to the second, then the third. Each page was blank. She was fanning through flashing white pages when she heard the front door lock flick open.

People Aren't Home

Alana sat in the armchair by the laundry machine, watching Sean stalk a spider. The cat hunted bugs. Spiders, ants, flies, wasps, moths. He would jump and slam his face into walls.

Janie spilled some soupy substance on her shirt. Alana handed her a damp cloth to clean it, but it didn't really work, just smudged it around.

Alana found four ants in the closet while grabbing a sweater. She called Sean in. Alana was sick of bugs and needed to get out of the apartment.

The girls argued and blamed each other for the bugs. Janie left, and a few minutes later, Alana walked out the door. As Alana walked away, she thought of Sean alone, resting his chin on his paw.

Jewellery Box

"Can you explain what happened here?" asked Alana.

"What are you talking about?"

"Did you break my jewellery box?"

"No." Janie stared at her phone.

"Who did, then?"

"It was probably Sean." Janie looked up at her sister from the couch, then returned to scrolling through her Instagram feed.

"Sean is sleeping and has probably been in the same spot all day."

"Okay, well, I don't know, Alana. It was like that when I got home."

"My jewellery box magically broke when you were the only person here."

"How do you know that?"

"Because no one else lives here!"

"And what about Sean?"

"Stop trying to blame the cat. He can hardly get on the dresser."

"Maybe he tried and accidentally knocked it off while falling."

The girls smiled at each other, the thought of Sean's jump, the attempt, the fall.

Blend

Alana put oats in the $15 blender, watched it whine and shake, felt it heat up. She was pleased with how the oats rendered into flour. She had to add more oats because she hadn't realized the contents would shrink when blended. She dumped the oat flour into a bowl of melted coconut oil and peanut butter, put almond slices into the blender. Watched as nothing moved. She consulted the vegan, gluten-free cookbook that her mother gave her as a gift even though she does not eat a vegan or gluten-free diet, read the same passage she'd read before, which doesn't say anything about what to do when using a cheap, shitty blender. She shook the blender, then pressed the button again. Watched as some of the almonds collapsed into a powder in the middle of the cup, then as the blades froze. She shook the blender, tried again.

Blue Nail Polish

Alana sat cross-legged on her bed, dipped the brush in the nail polish bottle on her nightstand after each nail to collect enough blue for the next. The polish was old, so she'd added a few drops of nail polish remover and had shaken it up to make it smoother, less clumpy.

She heard the door unlock, Janie's voice spilling into the apartment, "We have a cat—sorry, I should've mentioned that. I hope you're not allergic—" Sean meowed loudly. "Hi, Sean!"

Then a man's voice. "Oh, a little, but I'll be fine."

Alana knew Janie had a date tonight—some dude from one of her classes—but she had no idea she'd be bringing him here. Alana's bedroom door was closed so she kept it that way, hoped Janie would remember their rule: if you have a boy over, put some music on in your room to drown out any noise. Alana heard Janie and the boy make their way to Janie's bedroom, giggling and whispering, and the click of the door closing. She heard Sean scratching relentlessly to get in after Janie.

"I can't stop thinking about you," the boy said. Alana felt herself blush. "I keep thinking of those sounds you make."

"Oh..." Janie stammered, and then Coldplay filled the room, just loud enough so Alana couldn't hear any more of their conversation. Alana thought of the girl who had sat across from her in linguistics class before she'd dropped it, the one who bit her nails all the way through every tutorial, her "Green Eyes" like the song. Alana had been nervous to talk to her. Her bright eyes flashed up at the TA every time they asked the class a question, and Alana always wondered if she knew the answer but was too shy to raise her hand.

Alana opened her bedroom door a crack so Sean could come in. She dipped her brush in the blue, painted the next nail.

Rob in Real Life

TODAY 12:26 AM

he keeps sending me naked pictures of himself.
what does it mean Alana???

uh I dunno Sara I think it means he likes you
did u really have to go sit in a toilet stall to tell me this?

but why wouldn't he just say that
instead of sending nudes
it's a bit awkward don't you think

well yeah it is
I guess it means he wants you to see him naked
or wants to see you naked

I guess so. that makes sense

u send any back?

yeah :)
lol what do you think I'm doing right now

haha in a gross bar washroom???
I thought you had to pee!
who's that other guy then

who?

the one you've been flirting with here all night!

oh I don't know him he just started talking to me
ugh I wish I didn't have my period
I feel so gross and sweaty

haha aww
but what about Rob?
you've been letting this guy buy you drinks and stuff

who am I to tell him no!

okayyy

don't judge me Alana

I just think it's kind of mean that you're blatantly using him

he doesn't need to know that

I feel like an idiot sitting here by myself for so long
and I really want to smoke

you should have come with me
we could have had this conversation irl

are you almost done in there
your new friend is trying to talk to me now

yeah just peeing!

ugh
the bro next to him is showing him a nudie of some girl

ew
boys are gross

I Can't Find My Keys

TODAY 3:14 AM

you got drunk with Sara??

yes Janie
please let me in! I'm cold

man, Alana she's not a nice person

yes I know I'm sorry
she sucks
but it's all gooood
she's not coming over or anything
can you please let me in???

why should I??
I don't want to associate with friends of that asshole.

okay but
I'm your sister and I live here
and it's cold out and I really have to pee
let me in!

Alana

please!!!!

I'm not okay with this

I'm gonna pee my pants

just because you have some kind of lesbian crush on her
doesn't mean you get to hang out with my enemy

okay Janie come on
all she did was talk about herself the whole time
open the goddamn door

Away from Me

Scott told Alana to sit down. Just for two minutes. Before she made any rash decisions. The idea was that two minutes would turn to four, and so on. Janie had just stormed out of their apartment, still angry from the night before. Scott came over and put the kettle on to make Alana some morning tea. He said he liked to wait it out a bit when he was angry, so she should do the same. Alana sat at their white plastic table, a hand-me-down from their nonna. She tried to focus on the calming pattern of the matching chairs—the white frame, black cushiony bit with white spots. She focused on her breath, in and out. She used to kneel on the chairs as a kid so she could see above the table while her nonna sewed up holes in her nonno's pants, hummed while he drummed a beat on another plastic table upstairs.

"How're ya feeling?" She felt his hand materialize on her shoulder.

"Uh, better I guess."

"What kind of tea do you want?"

"Earl Grey."

"I think you should wait to call her until later," he said, digging through the tea cupboard. "Maybe tomorrow. I just don't want you to say anything you'll regret."

He plucked the tea bag out of the wrapper, dropped it into the mug, poured water from the kettle.

"What's waiting 'til later gonna do?"

"It'll give you time to think about what you want to say. She's obviously upset."

He poured milk into the tea, placed it on the table. Put the teabag in the compost. Sat on the couch, turned on a video game.

The Good Cheese

Alana bit into her vegetable cracker and the slice of brie on top. Dropped a few crumbs on the counter. Sean watched from her feet.

Janie walked into the kitchen, curled her lip. "Why does it smell like a dirty cloth in here?"

Alana paused her crunching. "Don't know," she mumbled.

Janie picked up the red dishcloth hanging from the faucet, sniffed it. "This is disgusting."

"Okay well it's not my fault!" Alana stuffed the cracker tube back into its box. Sean rubbed against her shins. She noticed a tiny piece of brie rind on the counter and pushed it towards the edge, looked at Sean. Sean stood on his hind legs, reached up towards the counter. She let it fall to the floor and he wolfed it down as she finished eating the other half of her cracker and the last bit of cheese.

"Is that the good cheese that Mom gave us?" Janie asked.

"... yeah," Alana answered, mouth full. Sean licked his paw and wiped his face, looked up at Alana.

Janie rolled her eyes. "If you're going to be home all day maybe you can, I dunno, do laundry or something?"

Alana sighed, "Yes, mother," and walked out of the kitchen.

Scraps

Alana sat on a hill in Trinity Bellwoods long enough for her jeans to feel wet on the butt. Stood to eat the rest of her falafel wrap. Leaves bunched up like pillows under trees but she resisted the urge to sit on them. She scanned through raindrops for the albino squirrel before remembering he'd died this summer. A photograph by someone in the neighbourhood was published in the *Star* as proof. Found hanging by his teeth from an electrical wire. She felt his absence the way she might feel for a favourite mug, reaching halfway to grab it before remembering it had broken, the pieces thrown out.

She wondered if they gave the squirrel to a museum. She sat on a wet picnic table and as she took the last bites of her falafel, she saw a white ribbon dash through the trees, dance in the branches and disappear. She squinted through leaves, over people wearing hoods and sitting on wet grass in circles, through the fence and trees around the dog park bowl. The flash was gone.

A few bits of her pita fell on the grass and some pigeons ambled in to gobble up the scraps.

Sparkling Pieces

Alana tried to catch her breath. The crystal vase from their nonna lay shattered in the sink. She was attempting to wash it while deflecting Janie's nagging when it slipped out of her hand. They stopped yelling, looked at the damage.

"Good job, genius." Janie rolled her eyes.

The apartment smelled of cat piss and there were few dishes not dirtied.

"You know what your problem is? You really need to grow up. You should maybe try actually sticking out school for a while."

"Because that's helped you so much," Alana mumbled, shifted the sparkling pieces of vase back and forth with her finger.

Janie found a can of tuna and some crackers in the cupboard and began to trawl around the cutlery drawer, pulled a spoon out from the mess of dollar store silverware. She walked to the kitchen table with Sean trailing close behind.

Janie should be leaving for class soon, Alana thought. She breathed in, held it. Flicked a few crumbs on the counter. Let her breath out, picked up the broken glass.

Dahlias

Alana's phone vibrated through her bag against the tree so she turned the buzzer off. Scott kept texting her, telling her to head to his place, but she wanted to stay out. Alana and Sara sat in the cool grass in the park and drank cider. Sara hid her can in one of her fuzzy blue socks, her feet bare, and Alana had hers shoved up her long sweater sleeve. Clusters of nighttime picnickers sprinkled the field around them. The dahlias on Sara's dress scrunched and stretched with her body as she spun on the grass and Alana couldn't understand why no one else was mesmerized.

why don't you come over now? he said. *I miss you.*

See If Your Heart Can Smile

The swampy air struck her face as Alana walked into the room, sweat beading instantly on her face and bare arms. Another woman lay on a bright pink mat, sprawled in her purple leggings and top. Looked as though she could have been napping. Alana wasn't sure what to do so she spread her body across her sticky mat and felt sweat leak from her armpits and where her butt met her thighs.

A man walked into the room, baggy pants and no shirt, muscly and soft at the same time. He stopped at the top of her mat and Alana contorted her neck to look up at him. He held his hands in a prayer-like position near his chest.

"Welcome, I don't think I've met you before," he said.

She smiled. The man walked up to the wall covered in mirrors and turned to face them.

"Hello, ladies," he said, "it looks like it's just going to be the three of us today." He spoke softly and she began to drift off, humidity clogging her ears. "... so why don't we start in savasana, or corpse pose, since you're both there already. Allow the heat into your muscles, feel it entering every pore. Forget about the stresses you held coming into this room. Try to let that go for the next hour."

As she lay glued to the mat by her sweat, Alana thought about the things she wanted to forget—Scott texting her every fifteen minutes and Janie telling her she needs to grow up. She tried to let them go.

"Feel your body getting lighter."

She did feel like she might be getting lighter, negativity sucked away, dripping out onto the floor.

"See if your heart can smile."

She tried for a second, still splayed on the ground. She tried to get her heart to smile.

Her Oversized Sweater

Wind blew through the wool of Alana's sweater as she walked across the bridge. She carried a bottle of wine in a paper bag and wished she could warm up that hand in her pocket. A man who looked like her uncle in a red and purple sweater stopped to take a picture of trees along the riverbank, their yellowing leaves. He looked at her as she got nearer, so she stared at the sidewalk.

"Stay warm."

She looked up and smiled, kept walking. He trailed after her.

"Are you in school?"

"I'm just taking some time off, hopefully next year."

"What will you take?"

"Writing, maybe."

"Cool! I write a bit, now and then. What's your name?"

"Um, Alana." She wasn't sure why she told him.

"Nice to meet you, Alana. I'm Andrew." He put out his hand to shake hers and she accepted. He held her hand a little too long. *You're being paranoid*, she thought.

"By the way, you have beautiful eyes," he said. She watched concrete rise under her shoes. "Maybe we could meet up for a coffee sometime and I could show you some of my stuff? I'd love to get your opinion."

"I guess," she said. *No*, she thought.

He went on about an experience he had while travelling in Thailand that he felt compelled to write a novel about.

"What's your phone number?" He pulled out his phone.

"I... don't have one right now." She didn't make eye contact.

"You don't have a phone number?"

"No."

"Well... do you have an email?"

"Um, yeah."

He handed her his phone and she typed her email address, erased it, typed it again. She immediately began to plan the moment when she received his email. She would block him. She regretted giving her actual email, she should've made one up.

He walked the same way as she did and said he was going for coffee now, did she want to come? No, she said. She was meeting a friend. She hoped he didn't follow her home. He offered to walk her there as they reached the coffee shop.

"No, thanks." Luckily the light changed then so she ran across the street.

She could see out of the corner of her eye, as she hustled away, the man still standing where she left him. She hugged her bottle of wine as the pigeons flew in circles above her, searching for somewhere to land.

Nothing

TODAY 2:43 AM

Can you answer your phone Alana?
I know it's late
I need to ask you something

Scott ...
it's 3 in the morning!!

Sorry
I just needed to ask you about tomorrow

about what
it can't wait till tomorrow?

I guess it could

...
I'm putting my phone on silent now

Sorry
Nothing
It was nothing

dude u have to stop doing this

Mirrors

Alana floated her hand above the doorknob as an insect with a hard shell scuttled along the wall. A scattering of four, five, maybe six brown bugs around the door. Smaller ones light brown, darker the larger they got.

"What's the matter?" Scott grabbed the doorknob and yanked the door open. Sound boomed from the speakers and ricocheted through the room. Blue lipstick and half-shaved heads. A living-room-turned-dance-floor. Aaron was playing DJ for the night behind a pile of black boxes and equipment, hair ironed straight. Scott ditched his coat in a pile beside the couch and turned in the small space to talk to Alana. She clutched her coat and bag in her arms.

"Why don't you put your stuff with mine?"

"I... did you see?"

"What?"

She looked around to make sure no one was close. "They have cockroaches," she yell-whispered.

"Well, jeez, Alana—it's weird if you carry your shit around. Just put it on top of mine. Want a drink?"

"I'm gonna smoke. We can go on the roof, right?"

Scott frowned.

Alana slid her arms into her coat sleeves and made sure not to let them touch any walls as she hurried back out to the hallway. She saw herself in the mirrors on either side of the elevator, checked her blue jacket for crawling things, pushed the button.

"Are you going up to the roof?" Aaron flowed out of the apartment after her, his coat brushing the walls and doorframe as his reflection lurched into the mirrors by the elevator. "I'll join you!"

Alana smiled at his reflection but all she could think was

cockroaches. She scurried onto the elevator and he followed her in, pressed "16."

As they stepped out onto the top floor, he popped a cigarette into his mouth and let it hang on one side while he shouldered open the door that led to the rooftop.

"Need a light, m'lady?" Alana pulled her coat tight around her while Aaron lit their cigarettes and put an arm over her shoulder. "You get so much wind up here."

"Yeah it's freezing." Lights flashed in the streets below as their smoke floated over the edge of the building.

Aaron squeezed her shoulders when she shivered and got behind her to use both hands, biting down on his cigarette. "You feel tense, girl." He began massaging her shoulders, migrating down her back.

Alana felt chills as she debated making a run for the door, but then it opened and Aaron pulled his hands away.

"Hey! I thought you'd be done by now," Scott said.

"I was just about to come in." She threw the end of her cigarette in an old coffee tin, marched towards Scott and lashed her arms around his waist, held on.

"Y'all are so cute," Aaron said, leaning on the rail protecting him from the several hundred feet of air and the concrete glittering from the evening's rain. Scott laughed. Aaron muttered something and stumbled inside.

"Can we go home?" Alana asked Scott. "The bug thing is really freaking me out." She held Scott, imagining the cockroaches inside his coat, crawling into his shirt.

All in Your Head

"Please sleep," he said at 4 am. Alana shivered, turned to face one way under the covers then back the other way. Sean shifted, curled on top of her feet. "It's all in your head. It was just a bad dream, babe," Scott tried to soothe her. It wasn't working. "The birds are already awake and I don't want to watch another movie. I'm tired." She twisted under the blanket, tried to arrange the layers. "Just close your eyes," he said. "Please sleep."

Flicker

He wrote *I miss you* in a text and she didn't know how to respond because she didn't miss him, so she wrote *aww:)*. He wrote *I love you*. He wrote *people always leave*. She did not want to be a blindfold over his eyes. He said *don't you believe me? I feel like you don't believe me*, and she pretended her phone was dead. She didn't want to hurt him. She couldn't say the words. She thought if he hated her it would be easier for them both. *please believe me*, he said, and her screen blinked with each message, and as his blindfold slipped *please believe me* became *you abandoned me* and *I needed you* and *I'll always remember your kindness*.

Snowflakes

New snow sparkled on the sidewalk as Alana walked home from work, downtown loud with Thursday's student crowds. She reached up her jacket, without undoing the zipper, and awkwardly untucked her black shirt from black dress pants to relieve the pressure on her belly. Slid her hand down the rail on the stairs to her basement apartment entrance. Dug in her pockets, her bag. No jingling. Her keys weren't there. She banged on the door, rang the doorbell. Tried phoning her sister but her phone was always on silent so of course she didn't answer. No movement except flashing lights from a movie. She tried to squint through the curtains their mother put up for them when they moved in, pressed her ear to the door. She saw Sean pacing in front of the door. At least he knew she was there. Heard dinosaur noises, people screaming for their lives. *Jurassic Park*. Janie had another date with that boy tonight—she must've brought him home after. Alana rang again, leaned her head on the door, waited. Janie's room was at the other end of the apartment with no window to knock on. Alana sighed. She tried ringing again, banged on the door a bit harder this time. Tried calling again and sent her a text. She pulled her coat down as far as it would go over her butt and sat on the cold bottom step to wait, watched snowflakes land on the railing, the grey concrete.

Blueberries and Bananas

Janie kept telling Alana how awful she felt about the night before, and Alana kept assuring her it wasn't so bad. Twenty minutes really isn't that long, and it wasn't too cold. Janie had shooed the boy out early in the morning and made pancakes for her sister. Sliced some bananas and put them on the table with maple syrup, cooked blueberries into the pancakes. She made a few tiny pancakes for Sean, who wasn't interested. He sat next to his food bowl and stared at Janie.

"Stop looking at me like that, Sean. You already had your food."

Sean meowed.

Janie went back to flipping the pancakes.

"You seem chipper this morning," Alana said, sipping her coffee.

"I wanted to make you a nice breakfast. And when's the last time we had pancakes!" Janie flipped a giant one which landed on a smaller one, and she tried to pry it off gently.

"The dude seems nice. He didn't say much," Alana said, "but, you know."

"Yeah, I guess he's nice, I don't know. I'm not sure if he likes me really."

"I mean... I definitely think he likes you."

"Okay, well I know he likes sleeping with me. But I don't know if he really likes me as a person."

"Do you like him as a person?"

"I don't know."

"Does he like *Jurassic Park*?" Alana asked, concerned.

"Well... we didn't watch much of it. And it was my idea, he just sort of went along with it."

"Hmmm. I don't trust him."

Janie flipped the last pancake. "Have you met anyone new lately?"

"No." Alana sat down at the table. She thought about Victoria after work, the red wine in her smile. About Carlos dancing at the bar. "I dunno. Everyone sucks."

"Everyone doesn't suck," said Janie. "You have to give people a chance."

Janie placed the plate piled high with pancakes in front of Alana at the table, blueberry juice oozing from each one. Alana looked down into her coffee cup, swirled the dark brown at the bottom.

Caps

Alana sat in an overpriced coffee shop, two empty espresso cups in front of her while she debated ordering a third. She watched the second hand drag on the black and white clock on the wall, a cartoonish painting of a steaming mug of coffee hung beside it. She considered waiting another five minutes, maybe ten, when her blind date—some guy from one of Janie's classes—rushed in and tried to say something, but it came out as a gurgle. He adjusted his hat and said, "The shop next door is pretty cool."

"I'm also late for things sometimes," she said. They smiled and he sat down. "Do you want an espresso or something? I had two while I was waiting."

"I'm really sorry, I just really wanted to see that place next door." He offered his hand. "Want to go check out another shop?"

She reached out as if to touch his hat then thought better of it. "I hate when people are late."

Thursday to Sunday

She left work and walked through the alley like she did every night. Three dudes stood near the far end, where the alley met Queen Street. She thought they might work in the theatre too, maybe as technicians.

These weren't those dudes.

They looked at her and murmured as she neared. She tried not to make eye contact, checked her phone, and tried to call her mother even though she knew she'd be asleep. Voicemail. Should she run? Look for some sort of weapon? She wished she had her pocketknife in her bag. There was a dumpster close by, maybe she could find something in there to protect herself, but what if it was empty?

She just kept walking. She shouldn't have to cower in the presence of a group of random dudes.

"Hello," one of them said. She looked up and he was smiling and the other two were still talking. She must've given him a shocked look because his eyebrows tilted up in concern. She smiled back and picked up her pace.

Pieces

Alana placed the kettle on the stove and turned it on, took the coffee tin out of the freezer and measured six tablespoonfuls into the French press. She opened the cupboard and reached for her mug but couldn't feel it there. She stood on her toes, groped around farther back—nothing. She looked in the dish rack—not there. In the sink, her favourite mug sat dirty, filled with water muddied by remnants of Janie's morning coffee—instant with sugar and skim milk. Alana felt rage bubbling in her stomach. Or was that hunger? Without food or coffee in her system yet, suddenly she was sobbing. She tried to wash her mug but her vision was blurred. She felt for the dish soap next to the faucet and accidentally knocked the crumb-covered plate Janie left on the counter onto the floor, a cracked piece shooting toward Sean, who jumped and arched his back. Alana could see that Janie had no respect for her. She constantly stole her clothes, left dirty dishes around, judged her for leaving school. Sean stared as Alana knelt and squinted, picked up each broken piece.

Second Favourite

Janie got home from class and Alana was sitting at the kitchen table, painting her nails and drinking tea out of a plain white mug. Sean meowed at Janie as she walked in, rubbed against her legs and darted over to his food bowl as if he hadn't eaten all day even though Alana had fed him twenty minutes ago.

"What colour are you doing?" Janie asked, eyeing Alana's nail polish bottle.

"My second favourite," answered Alana.

"Oh... which one's that?"

"Which mug did you use this morning?"

"I don't know... one from the cupboard?"

"Yeah, which one?"

"I can't remember, Alana, why does it matter?"

"It's almost like you have no idea how disrespectful you are."

"What are you talking about?"

"Are those my socks?" Alana couldn't take her eyes off her brand-new socks on Janie's feet, a gift to herself after realizing most of her other socks had holes in the heels.

"I... yes, I'm sorry. All of mine were dirty and you left these on the dryer..."

"Please take them off."

"Alana, come on you're being ridiculous."

"Take them off now."

"Okay! I don't know why you're so upset."

Sean bumped his forehead against Janie's shin, the grey of his fur the same colour as her socked feet.

echoes of silence

We All Fall Down

The oasis of mismatched couches and chairs held the audience tightly as Alana struggled to hear what the man at the front of the room above the bar was saying. Beer glasses smashed below, people yelled at a hockey game on TV. He was performing a monologue, holding a purse prop hostage, trying to talk an invisible person out of leaving. She swivelled to check the stairs. The chair came out from under her, but it was broken anyway, and the actor kept trying. Alana watched Janie climb the stairs, pay her entry, and turn her raptor eyes on her, as if she knew where she was. Janie might've thrown something but maybe it was the broken chair falling. Maybe Alana was falling on purpose because she knew it would happen anyway and she likes being over-prepared. Maybe it could've been avoided. Maybe Janie wasn't there, her eyes hadn't found Alana, and the chair hadn't collapsed. Maybe it wasn't broken. Maybe there was no game. Maybe Alana was just sitting and listening.

Lemons

Alana took several steps into the theatre. Sixth-graders in the audience shrieked a blend of French and English and a video on the wall sputtered people squeezing lemons between their teeth, letting sour juice spill over their chins as they shook their heads, snarled and snapped their teeth like dogs fighting over steak. She looked at her phone and there were no messages, nothing. A fellow usher, also dressed in black, urged her to hurry up. Grade eight girls sat in the front row with their feet on the stage. From her seat in the last row she wondered what would happen if someone fell from the balcony above her. The babble around her cranked up several decibels and her phone felt larger in her pocket and she wondered how many people might die if someone fell, one or two. The lights dimmed and the chatter stopped, and five dancers crawled onto the stage on all fours and snarled and spat at the audience while angry music slashed the air.

All Yours

Daisies leaned wilting on Victoria's coffee table, an empty wine bottle as a vase. Maybe it was something about the room but Alana felt lightheaded. Victoria drifted around, still in her black work clothes, filling their glasses of wine each time they drained them. Alana looked down at her grey socks floating above the beige carpet. She wasn't sure why she got so mad, was so mean to her sister.

"You can crash here if you want," Victoria said, "the couch is all yours."

Alana smiled from where she sat, sprawled across half the couch. She watched Victoria's frizzy hair float back and forth as she spun into the kitchen again for more snacks. Victoria brought out a plate of crackers and orange cheese, slid it on the coffee table. A cracker slipped off the plate. Victoria walked over to the tall window, taller than her, tapped it with her finger. Red, orange, yellow lights from the street glowed around her.

Unsettle Me

Morning light through the curtainless window woke Alana up. She shifted on the couch, picked up *The Cinnamon Peeler* from the coffee table, munched the stray cracker beside it. Rose after a few poems, stretched all the way to the kitchen. Washed her wine glass carefully. Victoria wandered in and leaned against the wall, stared into the sink.

"Do you mind bringing that plate in? I can wash it," Alana said.

Victoria sauntered over to the coffee table, brought the cheese plate remnants to the counter. Ate the leftover crackers.

"Wanna go for a walk?" Victoria asked.

"In a bit, I wanna clean up your kitchen first."

"Just leave it, I can do it later."

"Don't worry, I'll do it!"

Victoria sighed, touched Alana's shoulder. Grabbed the yellow jug of water on the counter. Walked to the coffee maker. Dumped in some water.

512 West

Alana didn't look at anyone for the whole day. Not even the bus driver when he said hello. She dumped her change into the metal fare box and kept her eyes low.

She saw an old acquaintance on the bus, one that pops up on Facebook but she doesn't talk to. One that posts racist memes sometimes.

He said, "Hi, Alana!" She had earphones on with no music playing so pretended she couldn't hear him. His smile dissolved as he turned to stare at bus ads.

She filed onto the train with the crowd on the dusty platform and chose a pole to hold onto. Chewed every one of her nails, threw the little white bits on the floor. Some of her fingers bled.

Got off the train at St. Clair West and waited on the damp streetcar platform. A couple played guitars and people gave them change.

She didn't give them any change.

The streetcar took her west to her old apartment with Janie, who had found a new place nearby. She'd moved in with that boy from her class, the one who's allergic to cats. Stucco and glass flashed by, nothing but stucco and glass. She stepped off and walked down the side street, looked at the house, the basement window. Its weathered brick clashing with the buildings around it.

She looked at her fingertips, the blood drying, crusting over.

Brown Cardigan

Alana walked slowly through the rows of the theatre after the evening show, picking up crumpled programs, straw wrappers, and empty plastic cups discarded under seats. She found a whole granola bar beneath one, still in the wrapper. She held it for a second, debated before throwing it in the garbage. Her phone buzzed with a text from Janie.

TODAY 10:11 PM

hey do you have my green tank top?
the one you always stole?
I can't find it

I dunno I'll check when I get home

Alana knew exactly where Janie's tank top lay folded in her dresser, stolen when they moved out of their apartment. Janie still hadn't noticed her missing cardigan—the brown one. Alana felt guilty for holding these items hostage, but Janie never wore the brown cardigan anyway. Alana untucked her black shirt on the way out of the building. She slid her arms into the brown cardigan, did up a few buttons, shuffled into her raincoat. She clipped on her helmet, keyed open her bike lock, and began to roll home down the shiny streets.

Bay Window

Alana biked to her new apartment with Sean slung in a cloth carrier over her shoulder. She slouched under his weight, bent over the handlebars in the sun. Sean meowed from inside the bag at every swerve. She locked her bike to the fence in the backyard, felt sweat drip down the back of her shirt, and went inside and up to the third floor. She set the carrier down on the green rug in the small kitchen and unzipped the front to release Sean. He rushed out and began frantically licking his back. He itched his face, and then stopped suddenly, eyes widening. A bird chirped out the window.

"Dr. Lane says you're doing good, Sean! You're a healthy senior citizen."

Sean glared at her, began licking his paw.

"Want some wet food?"

Sean meowed, rushed to his bowl. Meowed again.

Alana forked a bit of the slimy food into Sean's metal bowl, a treat to hold him over until dinner. He deserved it after putting up with a bike ride and a vet appointment in one day. She resealed the can with the plastic cover and stored the leftover food in the fridge. Slumped onto the floral armchair by the window, her legs slung over its arm, and picked up her phone—no new messages, no emails, no notifications on Facebook. She put it down on the windowsill and closed her eyes, let her limbs relax, listened as the hum of the fridge started up. She felt Sean leap onto her lap, knead her stomach and lie down, his face so close to hers that she could smell his wet food breath. He licked her chin and purred.

"Thanks, buddy," Alana laughed. She scratched behind his ears and he closed his eyes and purred louder.

The rain started to tap on the window. They got home just in time.

Acknowledgements

I've had the privilege of being taught and supported by some phenomenal writing teachers. Thank you to Jeanette Lynes, for your tireless dedication to your students, including me. Thank you for always cheering us on and lifting us up! Thank you to Jacqueline Baker, for believing in me and guiding me towards discoveries I needed to make to move this project forward. Thank you to Priscila Uppal, for introducing me to writing flash fiction and encouraging me, and all of her students, to keep writing.

Thank you to Debra Bell, John Kennedy, and the team at Radiant Press, for taking a chance on this manuscript and making it into a real book with me (even in the midst of a pandemic!), and thank you to Elizabeth Philips, for your thoughtful, clever, and attentive edits!

Thank you to the editors and literary journals that first published some of the pieces in this book—"Tough Pants," "Dandelion," and "Black Hole" appeared in *The Feathertale Review*; "People Aren't Home" and "Flicker" appeared in *BAD DOG*; "Four Flutes" appeared in *Bad Nudes*; "Somewhere Near Danforth," "We All Fall Down," and "Janie's Cat" appeared in *antilang*; and "Lava Rug River, Wine Mountain" appeared in *Sewer Lid.*

Thank you to all of the kitties who inspired Sean, especially Max and Clark.

Thank you to those who helped in small or big ways throughout the writing process—by giving feedback, workshopping pieces with me, inspiring pieces, saying things like "I like that" or "I don't like that," housing me during various stages of the writing process, helping me get cheap plane tickets to fly around to the places I wrote, and teaching me how to be a writer—Courtney Loberg, Leah

MacLean-Evans, Dave Margoshes, Meaghan Hackinen, Brent McFarland, Isa Lausas, Lesley Kenny, Stephanie McKechnie, Julia Heximer, Monica Sass, Tamara Gell, Tea Gerbeza, Sarah Ens, Carley Mascher-Mayson, Shannon McConnell, Lisa Bird-Wilson, Daniel Scott Tysdal, Catherine J. Stewart, Katherine Lawrence and Saskatoon Public Library's Writer in Residence program, Karen Solie and Memorial University's Writer in Residence program, Tara Dawn Solheim and Caitilin Terfloth at Sage Hill Writing and my wonderful fiction group there, the Saskatchewan Arts Board, the MFA in Writing at the University of Saskatchewan, Jenn Hogan and Dan Sumner, Heather and Jeff Migel, Myra Sheppard and Papa Brian, my hilarious nieces—Amelia, Izzy, Juliet, and baby Z—Nicole Di Cintio, my nonna Concetta and nonno Calogero Santamaria, my zia Santa Maniaci, my zio Stello Basile, my parents Joanne and Matthew Haldoupis, my brother John Haldoupis, my sister Danielle Haldoupis, and Geoff Pevlin, for egging me on and being the best first reader, editor, and deadline enforcer, and for always coming up with fresh material.

PHOTO: GEOFF PEVLIN

Nicole Haldoupis is a queer writer, editor, and designer from Toronto. She's a co-creator and editor of *untethered*, editor of *Grain*, and co-founder of Applebeard Editions. Her work can be found in *Bad Dog Review, The Feathertale Review, Bad Nudes, (parenthetical), Sewer Lid, antilang*, and others. *Tiny Ruins* is her first book.